# Pilar Speaks Up

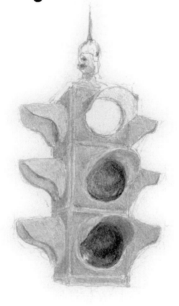

by Nomi Waldman
illustrated by Karen Jerome

 HOUGHTON MIFFLIN     BOSTON

S0-BCM-092

$\mathcal{P}$ilar liked school, and she was a good student. She thought her teacher was nice, and she got along well with her classmates. But Pilar had a problem. When it came to speaking in class or in front of a group, she was shy. It took great effort to get up the courage to speak, and even then her voice sounded faint. Like today, for instance.

"Speak up, Pilar," said Ms. Welch. "Maybe if you stood up, the class could hear you better."

Pilar could feel her face turn red. She stood up, repeated her answer, and sat down.

Ms. Welch nodded and went on to the next question from the social studies book. Pilar was so unhappy with herself that she tore her notes out of her notebook and wadded up the paper.

When the bell rang, Pilar grabbed her things, threw the crumpled paper in the trash barrel, and got out of the room as quickly as she could. She didn't even wait for K.T.

She was half a block from the school before she heard K.T. calling her. "Pilar! Wait up!"

"Hi," was all Pilar said, and kept on walking.

K.T. touched her arm lightly. "Wait."

Only then did Pilar look at her friend.

"I know what you're upset about," said K.T. "And if it helps any, I heard you just fine."

Pilar had to smile at that. After all, K.T. sat only a couple of seats in front of her.

They started walking again. K.T. kept talking. "Maybe it's Ms. Welch. Maybe she's going deaf or something. Oh—I'm sorry, Pilar, I forgot."

Pilar waved off the apology. It didn't embarrass her to talk about hearing loss just because both her parents were deaf.

Pilar shook her head. "No, it's me. I do speak softly. And I do need to speak up, but I'm not used to it and I'm kind of shy." At home, she didn't have to make any kind of sound when she spoke. Talking to her parents meant using sign language, something she'd been doing since she was little.

Pilar's own hearing was fine—almost too good sometimes. Maybe it was because the house was so quiet that she could notice the slightest sound wherever she went. Right now, for example, she caught the sound of little kids laughing and calling to each other. She looked around. They were half a block away, and traffic was noisy.

Pilar and K.T. were standing at the intersection of Main Street and Harwick Avenue. There was a crosswalk there, but the white lines were so faded that they were hard to see. With two-way traffic on Harwick, buses and trucks were always roaring by.

K.T. began telling Pilar about how she communicated with her grandmother, who was hard of hearing. But Pilar was only half listening. Over K.T.'s shoulder, Pilar watched a group of second-graders come running up, laughing as they pushed and bumped each other. One of them was Tobi, K.T.'s little sister.

Pilar knew that Tobi wasn't supposed to cross Harwick alone, but maybe the game was getting too rough for her. Pilar saw her start across, looking left, then right. But she didn't look left again, so she didn't see a van that was turning the corner.

"STOP!" shouted Pilar, putting all the force she could behind her voice.

Tobi heard her and froze. Even the van driver, with his windows open, must have heard, because he slammed on the brakes.

K.T. turned as Pilar shouted. Without hesitating, she grabbed her sister and pulled her back onto the sidewalk. As soon as she was sure Tobi was all right, K.T. looked at Pilar. She seemed shaky. "Thank you!" K.T. said.

"Thank you!" squeaked Tobi from inside the folds of K.T.'s jacket.

Then K.T. smiled and said, "Hey, I guess you can make yourself heard when you need to!"

That evening, Pilar told her parents about Tobi's near accident. Her hands practically moved in a blur as she rushed through the story.

"Oh, Pilar, I'm so glad you were watching that little girl!" Pilar's mother signed.

"You did the right thing," Pilar's father added. Then he touched her hand before he continued signing. "Sweetheart, you could be a leader. You are strong, and you have a good head on your shoulders. You must take advantage of other opportunities to speak up."

Pilar had a great deal to think about that night before she fell asleep.

When she got to the playground the next morning, Pilar found a group of her classmates talking excitedly. K.T. had just finished telling them what had happened the day before.

"There ought to be a traffic light at that intersection," Inez said.

"A traffic light—good idea," her twin sister Carmen echoed.

"But how do we get one put in?" asked Josette.

They all turned to Pilar as though she had the answer. "I—I don't know, but I suppose we could ask someone."

They waited for her to name the person.

"Well, maybe Ms. Welch would know," she finally managed.

After the last bell, Pilar and her friends approached Ms. Welch as a group. But Pilar realized that the others were expecting her to speak for all of them.

"Go on," hissed Inez, "ask her!"

"Ask her," echoed Carmen.

Josette and K.T. just nodded.

Pilar took a deep breath and began telling Ms. Welch what had happened and what the group thought should be done.

Ms. Welch listened closely, and her face grew thoughtful.

"Pilar, it's lucky that you were so alert," she said when Pilar had finished.

Again Pilar felt her face turn red, but it was a different feeling this time. She felt more proud than embarrassed.

Ms. Welch went on. "Perhaps the best approach would be to get people to sign a petition. Remember, we talked about petitions last week. If enough people sign it, we can present it to the school board so that they can act on it."

Ms. Welch's eyes swept the little group and came to rest on Pilar. The teacher smiled slightly. It was clear that she thought Pilar was the leader of the group. At the thought of being a leader, Pilar's first thought was to step back and let someone else do the talking. But then she remembered what her father had said. She smiled back at Ms. Welch.

It took a couple of days to get the wording of the petition just right. Ms. Welch helped Pilar and her friends to edit it. "Keep the message simple so that it's clear exactly what you want," she advised. "Then, when people read it, they'll understand right away and be ready to sign it."

At last they had the wording they wanted. Ms. Welch read the petition aloud: "We are asking that a traffic light be installed at the corner of Main Street and Harwick Avenue to protect the lives of schoolchildren trying to cross this busy intersection."

By the end of the week, the group had gotten most of the students in school to sign the petition. All the grownups signed, too, including the principal, teachers, and office and lunchroom staffs. Pilar herself went to several classrooms to explain the petition, and came back later to collect the signed forms. To her surprise, she found her confidence growing as she went from one room to the next.

Pilar's class even discussed the petition in social studies. Ms. Welch explained how necessary it was for citizens to speak up if they wanted action on an important issue.

"Now, the next step, of course, is that someone has to present the petition to the school board," she finished.

All eyes turned to Pilar.

Pilar caught her breath. Then she remembered what K.T. had said the day all this had started: "I guess you can make yourself heard when you need to!"

*Well, I need to be heard now,* she told herself.

Aloud, she said simply, "Yes, I'll go."